AMBER BROWN IS IN HOT WATER.

"Can I do extra credit?"

She shakes her head. "In this case, you may not. Extra credit's reserved for people who have tried their best and need an extra boost, or for people who are already doing their best and want to do more. YOU are not in either one of those categories."

She closes her marking book. "You have a chance to bring up your grade. Just make sure that you turn in all of your missing work."

I take the list of missing assignments that she hands me.

She continues. "Tomorrow, the class will be given a major project. Do well on it. I can't emphasize this highly enough. It will help bring up your grade for the marking period and will show me that you're serious about doing well."

I nod.

I, Amber Brown, may not be serious about a lot of things, but I am serious about this.

Paula Danziger

AMBER BROWN
WANTS EXTRA CREDIT

Illustrated by Tony Ross

PUFFIN BOOKS

Acknowledgments

*To everyone at the American School of
London—especially some of the most
terrific fourth graders ever (1994–95)*

To Bruce Coville—for listening

To the Evans family—Gill, Greg, Dan, and Isobel

PUFFIN BOOKS
Published by the Penguin Group
Penguin Young Readers Group, 345 Hudson Street, New York, New York 10014, U.S.A.
Penguin Group (Canada), 90 Eglinton Avenue East, Suite 700, Toronto, Ontario, Canada M4P 2Y3
(a division of Pearson Penguin Canada Inc.)
Penguin Books Ltd, 80 Strand, London WC2R 0RL, England
Penguin Ireland, 25 St Stephen's Green, Dublin 2, Ireland (a division of Penguin Books Ltd)
Penguin Group (Australia), 250 Camberwell Road, Camberwell, Victoria 3124, Australia
(a division of Pearson Australia Group Pty Ltd)
Penguin Books India Pvt Ltd, 11 Community Centre, Panchsheel Park, New Delhi - 110 017, India
Penguin Group (NZ), 67 Apollo Drive, Rosedale, North Shore 0632, New Zealand
(a division of Pearson New Zealand Ltd)
Penguin Books (South Africa) (Pty) Ltd, 24 Sturdee Avenue,
Rosebank, Johannesburg 2196, South Africa

Registered Offices: Penguin Books Ltd, 80 Strand, London WC2R 0RL, England

First published in the United States of America by G. P. Putnam's Sons,
a division of Penguin Young Readers Group, 1996
Published by Puffin Books, a division of Penguin Young Readers Group, 2008

5 7 9 10 8 6

Text copyright © Paula Danziger, 1996
Illustrations copyright © Tony Ross, 1996
All rights reserved

THE LIBRARY OF CONGRESS HAS CATALOGED THE G. P. PUTNAM'S SONS EDITION AS FOLLOWS:
Danziger, Paula, 1944–2004
Amber Brown wants extra credit / by Paula Danziger.
Illustrated by Tony Ross.
p. cm. Sequel to Amber Brown goes fourth.
Summary: Unhappy over her parents' divorce and her mother's boyfriend Max,
nine-year-old Amber finds her schoolwork suffering.
ISBN: 0-399-22900-0 (hc)
[1. Divorce—Fiction. 2. Schools—Fiction.]
I. Ross, Tony, ill. II. Title.
PZ7.D2394At 1996
[Fic]—dc20 95-586 CIP AC

Puffin Books ISBN 978-0-14-241049-3

Book design by Donna Mark.
Lettering by David Gatti. Text set in Bembo.

Printed in the United States of America

To Ben Danziger
Your book, with love from Aunt

AMBER BROWN
WANTS EXTRA CREDIT

Chapter One

★ ★ ★ ★ ★ ★ ★ ★ ★

AMBERINO CERTIFICATES

I, Amber Brown, being of sound mind and no money (I spent it all on a book, a computer game, and some junk food), do hereby give my mother five Amberino Certificates for her birthday.

Amberino Certificates allow The Mother (Sarah Thompson) to ask her beloved only child (Amber Brown) to grant her five wishes. . . . Just remember, these have to be wishes that I can actually do . . . . not stuff

1

like move the Empire State Building or eat spinach or find the cure for dandruff (not that you have it or anything). Just remember, I'm just a nine-year-old kid, so make the wishes doable . . . but then you always do!!!!!!!

HAPPY BIRTHDAY AND LOVE FROM

Amber Brown
♡ ♡ ♡

* * * * * * * * *

Chapter Two

I, Amber Brown, am being held captive by a madwoman.

That madwoman is my mother, and she's very mad at me for having a messy room.

She's also very mad at me because my teacher, Mrs. Holt, sent home a note saying that I'm "not working up to the best of [my] ability."

My mother is very, very mad at me because of the note. Actually what she said is that what she's very angry about is the reason for the note . . . . me not doing my schoolwork the way I should.

Now I'm supposed to be a perfect little student.

And she's using one of the Amberino Certificates to make me clean up my room.

She says that I can't leave my room until it's "neat as a pin."

How can a room be neat as a pin? Does a pin have a bed in it—a dresser, curtains, a person living in it?

The words "neat as a pin" are the second-silliest thing I've ever heard.

The first-silliest thing is expecting me to have a neat room.

I wish I never gave her those Amberino Certificates for her birthday.

Doesn't she know that if my room is neat, I can't find anything?

It makes me nervous if everything is too organized.

She never used to mind that my room wasn't neat.

She never used the Amberinos to make me clean it up.

The telephone rings.

I rush out to answer it.

My mother gets to it first, picks it up, and listens.

Then she says, "Brandi, I'm sorry, Amber can't come to the phone. . . . ."

"I'm at the phone. . . . I don't have to come to the phone." I pull on my mother's sleeve.

My mother points her finger at my room. "Back, Amber . . . . I'm serious. You have to clean your room before you do anything else."

"But Mom . . . ."

"No 'But Mom's,' " she says. "CLEAN YOUR ROOM . . . . NOW."

She starts talking on the phone. "Brandi, she can call you back as soon as her room is clean. . . . Yes, I'll remind her to bring her new game cartridge when she goes to your house tonight . . . if she gets her room organized by then, you will see her and the game. Otherwise, I'm not sure you'll see either."

I stomp into my room.

This isn't fair.

My room is a little messy, but I, Amber Brown, don't think she's really angry about my messy room.

I think that my mom is really angry because I don't want to meet her dumb boyfriend.

That's one of the big reasons why she's in such a bad mood.

Just because she wanted to use one of her Certificates to have me finally meet Max and go out to dinner with them . . . and just because I said, "No, I'm not ready yet, and you promised I don't have to until I'm ready. You promised that a long time ago . . . . so the Certificate can't make me go."

If I meet Max, I'll have to actually know that he's a real person . . . . a real person who is going out with my mom . . . . and if my mom is going out with him . . . . . that really means that there's less chance that she and my dad will get back together.

And what if I meet Max and actually like him? That wouldn't be fair to my dad, who's in Paris, France, which is so far away.

So, I'm not ready to meet Max, and I may never be ready.

I stomp some more and then I start throwing things into garbage bags . . . . . .

my dirty clothes, my clean clothes, the book report I've been working on for the last week.

And then I put the garbage bags in my closet.

Next, I put in all of the important things from the top shelf of my bookcase . . . the Dad Book that I keep so that I can look at pictures of my dad and talk to him sometimes . . . . the ball that Justin and I made from our used chewing gum . . . . the scrapbook that my aunt Pam and I made up of our trip to London. (It even has a chickenpox scab in it to remind me of how I got sick there.)

I open the top drawer of my dresser and shove everything on top into it.

I get into bed, and from under the covers, I start to make my bed, pulling up the sheets and then the blanket and then the bedspread . . . . then I get out and kind of smooth everything down . . . . the Amber Brown Way to Make a Bed.

Then I throw my stuffed animals on my bed.

I guess there's not only a madwoman in the house but a mad kid.

There's no madman in the house, though, because he, my father, and my

mother got so mad that they got divorced, and now he's in France because of his dumb job.

I, Amber Brown, wish things would go back to the way they were before . . . . before my dad left . . . . . before Justin, my first best friend, moved away . . . . . before my mother changed her last name back to the name she had before she got married so that we don't even have the same last name anymore . . . . before Max, the dumbhead boyfriend, met my mother . . . . before it was so important to get me to keep my room neat.

I wish.

Chapter Three

I'm escaping.

I'm out of the house.

My room passed inspection.

I'm really lucky that my mother didn't look in the closet or dresser drawers, or I would still be in my room instead of getting a ride to Brandi's sleepover.

My mother and I are in the car, not saying much of anything.

What she did say is that she is "really not happy with the way I've been acting."

Well, I'm really not happy with the way she's been acting.

I keep staring straight ahead.

Then I look over at my mother.

There are tears rolling down her face.

She hardly ever cries.

I've only seen her cry big time four times
. . . . . Once was when she got a call that
my grandfather, her father, had died . . . . .
and once was right after my father left. Even
though she'd said she wanted him to leave,
she still cried. And once I saw her cry when
I was about five and I ran out into traffic and
almost got hit by a car, but it stopped in
time. She yelled at me and then picked me

up, hugged me, and told me never to do that again. Then she told me how much she loved me and then she cried.

And now she's crying.

"Mom, what's wrong?" I touch her arm.

She pulls the car over by the sidewalk and looks at me. "Amber, it's so hard. I want to be a good mother."

"You are." I tell her that to make her stop crying and because even though I get mad at her, I know it's true.

She wipes her eyes. "And I want to be good to myself, too."

I sit quietly.

"You are making it very hard for me," she says.

I continue to say nothing.

"It's not all your fault," she says. "I've read all the books. Sometimes I'm even afraid that I'm beginning to sound like one of them. . . . . I understand that sometimes, many times, it's very hard for a child to accept the fact that parents divorce and then start dating other people. I understand . . . . . but I don't like it."

"I don't like it either," I tell her. "This isn't a book. This is my life. I can't help it if I want you and Daddy to stay together and for both of you to not go out with other people."

She sighs. "Your father is in France, doing whatever he wants to do, without your knowing, without your making it difficult for him."

I think about what she said.

Even though I don't want to admit it, she's right.

I say, "If I knew that he had a girlfriend, I'd tell him that I wouldn't want to meet her any more than I want to meet Max."

"But you don't even know, do you?" my mother says softly. "But you do know what I do because you live with me . . . . and, Amber, you know that I want you to live with me. . . . I'm not complaining or upset about that . . . I just want you to listen, to try to understand and to try to make things easier for me."

There are more tears rolling down her cheeks.

"I'll listen. I'll try." I hate to see her cry.

She continues. "We live with each other full-time. In some divorce families, children spend some time with each parent, and that allows the parents some time to themselves.

We're not, at present, a family that can do that. So you know a lot about what I do and who I spend my time with."

"So . . . ." I ask, "what do you want me to do?"

She takes a deep breath. "I want you to understand that I need to get on with my own life, to meet new people and include these new people in my life . . . . in our lives."

"New people . . . . you mean Max." I look at her.

She nods. "Especially Max. You know, Amber, it's not as if I'm asking you to meet an ax murderer. Max Turner is one of the nicest men I've ever met. He's a good man, funny and gentle and kind."

"Are you going to marry him? Are you going to expect me to call him Dad?" Now I feel like crying.

She shrugs. "I don't know if I'm going to marry him, but I do know that I like him a lot . . . and, no, I don't expect you to call him Dad. You already have a father. You can call him Max."

"Max," I say softly, thinking about how I once knew a Max, but he was a dog.

I wonder if I said, "Roll over and play dead" to Max the person, if he would do it.

I smile, thinking about making Max the person roll over and play dead.

My mother smiles back. "See, it's not so bad thinking about meeting him. You just smiled."

"I was thinking about the Hawkinses' dog, Max," I say in a mean voice, "and how they used to have him roll over and play dead."

My mother stops smiling and starts to cry again, just a little.

I really do hate it when she cries.

"Oh, okay," I sigh, and give in.

"Then you'll meet him? Promise?" She sounds happier.

"I promise to meet him. I don't promise to like him," I say, and think . . . . . *Okay, Max . . . . . roll over. Play dead.*

"It's a beginning." She smiles.

Chapter Four

"I'm going to kill my brother." Tiffani Shroeder pretends to wring an invisible neck.

"There are laws against that." Brandi laughs.

"What did he do this time?" I ask, dipping my potato chip into the onion dip.

Tiffani grabs a potato chip, puts it in her mouth, and crunches.

While she swallows, I smile, thinking about how much I like her five-year-old brother, Howie. He's very cute and does stuff that makes me laugh.

Tiffani eats a few more potato chips, while we wait for her to tell us what happened.

I look at Tiffani.

She has potato chip crumbs sitting on her chest.

If potato chip crumbs dropped on my chest, they would end up on the floor.

Tiffani Shroeder is the first girl in our class to have to wear a bra.

Hannah Burton wore a bra first, but she really didn't need one.

Tiffani speaks. "You know my Barbie doll collection? Well, you know that I don't play with them anymore. I mean, that would just be too baby. But they are my Barbies."

I wonder if since Tiffani changed the spelling of her name from y to i, she's changed the spelling of Barbie to Barbi . . . . I guess that her whole collection of the dolls, though, would still be Barbies. (I, Amber Brown, am very good at the spelling of plurals.)

Tiffani continues. "Well, that little runt and his little runt friends were playing with their X-Men toys and they decided to declare war. . . . . I came home and found my Barbies strangled with my grandmother's yarn and strung across the living room. Prom Barbie. Business Barbie. Lifeguard Barbie. College Barbie . . . . and all of the others. It was Barbicide," Tiffani says.

"Yuck. That's weird." Naomi makes a face.

Tiffani nods. "They also strung up all of the little runt's G.I. Joes."

"An Equal Opportunity Massacre." I shake my head.

Everyone groans, and Brandi empties the last of the potato chip bag on my head.

The potato chip crumbs fall off my head, onto my sweatshirt, and onto the floor.

Tiffani says, "One of the little runts even accidentally stepped on my book report and ruined it. Now I have to spend most of tomorrow redoing it."

I think about how my own half-finished book report is in one of the garbage bags in my closet. I'll have to fix mine up, too.

But tonight, while my mother and Max the person are out on a date, I, Amber Brown, am at a pajama party, having fun with my friends.

As for the book report . . . . . . It's Saturday night. I'll think about it on Sunday. After all, tomorrow is another day.

Chapter
Five

"We must . . . . . we must . . . we must . . ." Naomi and Alicia scream out of the car as Naomi's mother drops me off at my house.

I can't stop laughing.

I also can't stop hoping that they won't finish the cheer, which is "We must . . . we must . . . we must improve our bust. . . . We better . . . we better . . . before we wear a sweater." It's a cheer that the sixth graders do.

Last night we did jumping jacks to that cheer.

As far as I can tell, nothing much has changed about my body except that it's very tired.

No one gets any sleep at a sleepover.

Tiffani tried, but we kept whispering in her ear, "Beware your little brother. Today a Barbie doll . . . tomorrow a big sister."

I look at the driveway to see if there are any strange cars in front of my house . . . . To see if Max is there.

No car . . . . . no Max . . . . . . He's not in the house, either. . . .

Just my mother, sitting in the kitchen, drinking a cup of coffee.

"Did you have fun last night?" She smiles at me.

"I did." I pour myself a glass of milk and sit down.

"Mrs. Colwin let us use some of her old makeup and try on her jewelry. Can I get my ears pierced? And then we played Truth or Dare . . . . and we all had to name the boys we want as boyfriends."

My mother laughs. "Slow down, honey . . . . I can see that you put makeup on . . . . When you get older and are allowed to wear makeup, might I suggest that you don't outline your lipstick in green? . . . It's just a suggestion, though. Don't think I'm being critical."

I laugh, too. "It was dark. It was late. I

thought it was lipliner. It was eyeliner."

She continues to smile. "Amber Brown, you know we decided that you could get your ears pierced when you are twelve."

"Mommmmmmmm," I beg, "everyone is getting it done."

My mother raises one eyebrow.

I know that is a definite no.

I squint my eyes closed and stick out my lower lip.

She knows that is a definite pout.

Changing the subject, she says, "Who did you choose as a boyfriend, or did you take the dare?"

"The dare was that I would have to go up to Fredrich Allen in school on Monday and give him a kiss. He's the kid who picks his nose and chews it."

My mother makes a gagging sound and says, "Who did you say your boyfriend was?"

"I said it was Justin." I sigh, thinking about my best friend, who moved away at the end of the last school year.

"You really miss him, don't you." She ruffles my hair.

I nod.

It makes me sad to think that Justin is so far away and that he hardly ever writes to me.

It's not that he was really a boyfriend, he

was a boy friend . . . . but I said he was a boyfriend because I didn't want to kiss Fredrich Allen.

I do miss him.

He would understand why I don't want my mother to go out with Max, why I miss my father.

My dad used to take Justin and me to baseball games. He took us fishing. He took us to see the gory horror movies that my mother hates.

"Amber," my mother says softly.

"Yes?" I get nervous sometimes when my mother speaks very softly. . . . It's like she wants me to listen very carefully . . . . usually to something I don't want to hear.

"Amber . . . . remember yesterday when you said that you would be willing to meet Max? . . . Well, he's going to take us out to dinner tonight." She refills my glass of milk and then looks at me.

I have to figure out what I want to say, so I sit quietly for a minute.

"Mom . . . . . I said sometime . . . not immediately. . . . I have homework to do today. . . . . I have to think about it. . . . How about over Christmas vacation?"

"Amber." She shakes her head. "This is the beginning of October. We're not waiting until the end of December."

"My homework," I plead, knowing that she knows how important it is that I get it done.

She stares at me. "Do it now. You have all day to finish it . . . . and you know it better be done well. Max won't be here until around six o'clock. That gives you a lot of time. Now, Amber, you promised that you'd meet Max. I'll even use up two of the Amberino Certificates on this."

I stand up.

I know it's no use to argue.

And I started out having such a nice Sunday.

And then she ruined it.

Well, just wait till she sees what I'm going to do to hers.

Chapter Six

I stomp (all the way) up the stairs on the way to my room.

On the first step, I stomp because I have to meet Max. . . .

On the second, because I'm going to have to sit down at a table and eat dinner with him. . . .

On the third, because my mother is making me do this. . . .

On the fourth, because my father isn't here to see what's happening and get back together with my mother. . . . . .

I stomp with both of my feet on the fifth

step because my parents have changed my life without my permission. . . .

I stomp up the rest of the way because I know it will really annoy my mother and because my feet just want to stomp.

Then I slam my door.

My hands just want to slam.

I throw my knapsack on the bed and then I throw myself on the bed.

I lie on my bed and think about Max.

I just know I'm going to hate him.

I bet he looks like a gorillahead . . . or probably a gorillabutt.

I bet he's gross-looking, with hairs growing out of his nose and ears, and I bet that he smokes cigarettes and belches and blows his nose in the dinner napkin and then puts the napkin on the table . . . and I bet he hates nine-year-old girls.

I pretend one of my stuffed animals is Max. I choose the gorilla.

Pretending to be a ventriloquist, I put the

gorilla's face near mine. "So, Amber . . . I understand that you don't want me to take your mother out."

"That's right, banana breath." I stare at Maxgorilla.

The gorilla voice says, "Ha-ha, you lose. I'm a grown-up, and what I say goes."

I glare at Maxgorilla. "Who says, you foul fur-face?"

"I says . . . . and so does your mother. After all, she did make you meet me," the gorilla tells me.

I throw Maxgorilla across the room.

He hits the wall and falls into the garbage can.

Trying to calm down, I count to ten.

That doesn't work.

I count to twenty, thirty, fifty, one hundred.

That doesn't work either.

I try to think about all of the stuff I have to do.

That definitely doesn't work. Who can think about homework at a time like this?

I just can't calm down.

I get up and take out my Dad Book. Opening it up, I talk to my favorite picture of my dad.

I tell him what's going on.

I beg him to come home and try to straighten things out.

I say, "What happens if Max isn't so bad and I actually like him?" Will my dad hate me for liking Max, for going places with him and Mom?

I wish that my father would speak to me face-to-face, person-to-person, Dad-to-Amber. Hearing his voice once a week on the phone just isn't enough.

And it isn't easy for me to say some of this stuff into a phone.

I tell his picture this and ask him what he's going to do about what's happening.

But he's only a picture, so he doesn't answer; and I don't want to have to pretend to be a ventriloquist to make him say what I want to hear, so there's only silence.

It's so silent.

I'm screaming inside . . . . . and I don't know how to make anything come out.

Chapter Seven

I sit at the restaurant table, making a list of things that I, Amber Brown, don't like.

1. I don't like eating at restaurants. It's so boring . . . . waiting to get a table . . . . waiting to order something to drink . . . . . waiting for the waiter or waitress to come and take the order . . . . waiting for the dinner to arrive . . . . . waiting to order dessert . . . . waiting for the check.

   I personally think that not only the people who work at the restaurant should be called waiters, I think that the people who eat there should be called waiters, too.

   Take me to a fast-food restaurant anytime. You stand in a short line, or you even get to go through in a car. Everything arrives at once in a nice little box with your own packets of ketchup and stuff. You don't have to say, "Please, pass the _____." It's all there, and sometimes you even get a toy or something with it. And then you eat it and you're done. You don't have to sit around gabbing all day.

2. I don't like having to sit in a restaurant with Max, who I don't like.

3. I don't like complaining all the time, but what's a kid to do when nothing is going the way she wants it to go?

"Amber, please pass the salt." Max smiles at me.

I pass him the salt.

He could have just as easily asked my mother to pass him the stupid salt, but, no, he has to ask me.

"Thanks."

"It's nothing."

My mother starts to talk. "You know . . . . the two of you have a lot in common.

You both like to tell jokes. You both like to eat the center part of the Oreos."

Great, I think, *that'll be another thing we have to share.*

"You like to read. You like to travel. You like to see horror movies." She babbles on.

I look at Max. "My dad takes me to horror movies. He'll be taking me to a lot of them when he moves back here."

"Amber," my mother says softly.

Max says, "Well, maybe we can just see a few of them until he comes back."

"He can take me to all of them." I glare.

"Amber," my mother says again.

Max looks at my mother and says, "Sarah, honey, relax."

How dare he call her honey. That's what my dad used to call her before they started fighting. That's what my mom calls me.

He puts his hand on top of hers, and they hold hands at the table.

I accidentally spill my drink on the table.

While we wait for the waiter to clean it up, my mother tries to sponge up the liquid with her napkin.

She's no longer holding Max's hand.

I don't want to like Gorillaface, not for one single moment.

And he's acting so nice. He does seem like my mom said he would be. I hate it that he's acting so nice. This would be much easier if my mom WAS dating an ax murderer. Then I could really hate him.

Max and my mother are hugging.

I look over at my mother.

She and Max are kissing.

That's so gross.

I say, "Mom, I hope that the fungus in your mouth is getting better."

And then I look at Max and smile. "The doctor says that in girls it's curable. Boys die from it."

"Amber," my mother says, "stop that."

Max laughs.

I hate it.

He really doesn't even look like a gorilla. He's got dark hair, brown eyes, and he smiles a lot.

My mother continues. "You both like to chew gum. You'll have to show Max your chewing gum ball sometime."

Max pretends to take out a stick of gum, put it in his mouth, blow a huge bubble, and pop it all over his face. He pretends to wipe it off.

I will not smile at Max.

I will not smile at Max.

I will not smile at Max.

I will not smile at Max.

I will not smile at Max.

Chapter
Eight

Mrs. Holt collects all of the book reports
. . . . . all of them except for mine and Eric
Feinstein's.

Eric's not in school today because he
broke his arm over the weekend.

Some kids will do anything to get out of
doing their homework.

I know Eric didn't do it intentionally, but
he's lucky that he's got a real excuse . . . . .
and he's unlucky that he's got a broken arm.

I wonder if he broke the arm he writes
with.

I wonder if I should have made up a list

of excuses, or maybe I should have broken my arm, but I hate it when I even break my fingernail.

It's not really my fault that I didn't do my book report.

All Sunday I was too angry to work on my report.

When we got back from dinner, I told my mother that I had to go upstairs to finish my homework, but since Max didn't leave

right away, I had to sit silently and sneakily on the top of the steps, spying on them.

I thought I was doing a real good job of spying and listening until Max called out, "Do you want us to speak louder, Amber?"

Max thinks he's so funny.

So does my mother, because she laughed when he said that.

So I went into my stomp-and-slam routine, and then my mother came upstairs and told me that enough was enough, that she was trying to be patient with me but she'd had enough, and it was time for me to go to bed.

So I went to bed.

So it's really my mother's fault that I didn't get my homework done.

Mrs. Holt is calling out everyone in the class by name to take attendance and to have that person bring up the book report.

"Amber Brown." Mrs. Holt gets to my name.

Very softly, I say, "I'm here but my book report isn't. I'll bring it in tomorrow."

Someone goes, "Dun-di-dun-dun . . . . dun."

Someone else goes, "Not-done-di-done . . . . done."

Hannah Burton looks at me and smirks. "It figures."

I cross my eyes at Hannah Burton.

Mrs. Holt writes something in the marking book and calls out the next name.

It's just my luck that it's not a regular written-on-a-piece-of-paper report that can be passed up to the front without everyone knowing that you didn't do your work. But it's a book report that is supposed to be shaped to look like a cereal box.

I really did start mine. It was called *Anastasia Krupnik Krunchies* (it was about one of Lois Lowry's books). I'd already done the book summary that was supposed to go on the back, along with:

NUTRITION FACTS

Character Development   100%

Adventure   50%

Interest   100%

Personalities   100%

Dialogue   100%

Pictures   80%

Anastasia Krupnik Krunchies
contains the ingredients found only in
the best food for thought.

I knew what I was going to do for the front cover . . . . . . draw a picture of Anastasia and show that inside the box would be an author trading card. I was going to make up one about Lois Lowry, with facts and a Xeroxed picture.

So I did have a lot done, but I scrunched it up when I was mad and then never finished the report.

I read the book and loved it.

I did most of the work.

It's only a book report.

So what's the big deal?

Chapter Nine

"I can't believe you didn't do your book report. Amber, what's going on? You've been acting so weird." Brandi puts a tuna fish sandwich on her tray.

I take a sandwich and a bowl of red Jell-O.

I, Amber Brown, love red Jell-O. I love the way it squishes through my teeth while I'm eating it.

I, however, don't feel good about having to talk about why I'm acting so weird.

I try to make a joke about it. "People have always said that I'm weird."

Putting my tray down on the counter, I grab my ponytails and pretend they are motorcycle handlebars, and make engine noises.

Usually this makes her laugh.

This time it doesn't.

She does smile, though, and says, "That kind of weird is what I like about you . . . . This is a different kind of weird."

We continue to go through the line.

"You're in a lousy mood sometimes, and you're not as much fun as you used to be . . . . . and you won't talk about what's bothering you."

I pretend to have trouble making up my mind about whether to choose chocolate milk or regular milk.

Brandi sighs.

We pay for our food and sit down.

At the table on the right, some of the sixth graders are blowing straw wrappers at one another.

At the table on the left, some of the third graders are having a competition to see if they can make milk come out of their noses.

I unwrap my peanut butter, jelly, and banana sandwich and add some potato chips to it.

Naomi and Alicia join us.

So does Hannah Burton.

Having to sit next to Hannah Burton is enough to make me lose my lunch . . . and I'm not talking about misplacing it.

She takes out her lunch, which she's brought from home.

It's Chinese food, probably leftovers.

I love Chinese food.

But I would never ask Hannah to share it.

Hannah takes out a pair of chopsticks and starts using them.

She's such a show-off.

I love Chinese food but I hate chopsticks.

The only way that I don't drop everything when I use them is if I spear the food.

"Nice work, Amber. I can't believe that you didn't do your book report. Couldn't you find a book to match your interests? Did the library lend out the last copy of *Where's Spot?*" She picks up some cold noodles with sesame sauce on them and chopsticks them into her mouth.

"Are you enjoying your lunch? Worms with worm doodoo, isn't it? Mmmmmmm, good."

Hannah puts the chopsticks down for a minute, and then she picks them up again. "You are just so immature, Amber. Late growing up . . . . . . late turning in your homework."

I wonder what Hannah Burton would look like with chopsticks up her nose.

Seeing Hannah with the chopsticks reminds me of last year when our class studied China, and Justin and I dueled with our chopsticks.

Why couldn't Hannah have moved to Alabama instead of Justin? Maybe she could have even moved to China.

Tiffani Shroeder joins us.

She opens up her lunch bag, looks inside, and says, "I'm going to kill that little goofball."

"What is it? What has Howie done this time?" I know who she is talking about. "Goofball" is one of the cleaner things that Tiffani calls her younger brother.

Tiffani pulls something out of her lunch bag.

It's a Barbie doll wrapped in a piece of bologna. One of its arms sticks out through the bologna. The other arm sticks out of the top.

"It's Lunch Meat Barbie." I giggle.

"I'm going to get that kid." Tiffani shakes her head. "I don't know what I'm going to do, but I'm going to get him."

"Is that your whole lunch? Want some of mine?" I offer her half of my sandwich.

She looks back into the bag. "No, thanks. The little creep put this on top of the lunch that my mom made for me."

The rest of her lunch looks absolutely normal.

I was hoping that Howie had done more . . . . . like included Barbie-Q chips or something . . . but for a five-year-old he does pretty well.

We continue to eat and talk.

Hannah Burton drops *moo goo gai pan* on her sweatshirt.

I like lunchtime.

It's a good time for me to forget my problems.

The first bell rings, and we take our garbage and throw it in the bins.

As I walk back to class, I hear Mrs. Holt call out, "Amber."

I walk over to her.

She's very nice, but I just know that she's mad at me.

She says, "Amber, I would like you to see me after school before you go to Elementary Extension."

I nod.

I, Amber Brown, am in deep trouble.

Chapter
Ten

The end-of-the-day bell rings.

Everyone else gets up to leave.

I just sit there.

"I'll see you in Elementary Extension,"
Brandi whispers. "Good luck."

Hannah Burton smirks at me.

*Smirk. Smirk. Smirk. Hannah Burton is such
a jerk* is what I think.

Everyone else leaves.

It's me and Mrs. Holt, alone in the room.

My stomach hurts.

I, Amber Brown, never used to get in
trouble in school . . . . . not for grades and

not for not doing my work . . . sometimes for talking and giggling, but not for big stuff . . . . I don't know what's going to happen.

I walk up to Mrs. Holt's desk and wait until she's finished writing something in her marking book.

I stand there and look at the clock, waiting.

Something must be wrong with the clock. I feel like it's hours and I've only been standing here for minutes.

Mrs. Holt looks up.

"I'll turn the book report in tomorrow," I promise.

"Amber, bring a chair over and sit down here."

I get the chair and sit down by the side of her desk.

Her desk is so big. Her chair is so much higher than mine.

I look up, try to smile, and wait for her to say something.

She waits, too.

There really must be something wrong with the clock. It's ticking loudly, very loudly.

I can't stand the quiet. "Mrs. Holt. I promise I'll bring the book report in tomorrow."

"Amber, what are we going to do?" She puts down her pen and looks at me. "I've

sent a note home. Do you want me to start sending home worksheets with your assignments on them so that your mother can see them and sign them? Is that what you want?"

"No." I bite my lip and try not to cry.

She looks at her marking book. "You're missing assignments . . . . not just the book report, but three math homeworks, two essays . . . . and you've gotten low grades on several tests. And it's only October."

"Are you sure?" I ask, even though I know she's right.

"I'm sure." She nods. "Amber, I know you can do the work. I've checked your records, spoken to your old teachers."

"They're not so old," I say, and then I put my hand over my mouth.

I can't believe that I said that. It just came into my brain and out of my mouth.

She looks at me for a minute.

It's another very long minute, and then she smiles.

Mrs. Holt has a very nice smile, for a person who is probably going to flunk me.

Amber Brown. Fourth Grade Failure.

"Amber," she says.

"I'm sorry," I say.

Amber Brown. Sorry Person.

"As I was saying, I've been speaking with some of your past teachers."

I think . . . *And they passed me. . . . Please pass me too* . . . . but I don't say it out loud.

"You know, Amber, when I spoke to Mr. Cohen, he told me what he'd written in your 'Passport to Fourth Grade' . . . . how he loved your sense of humor, your sense of exploration . . . how you're willing to try out new things even when they're hard. I've been able to see some of that, but I'd love to see more of it . . . . and more of your homework assignments."

We smile at each other.

"Amber, I know you can do the work. What's wrong? Is it anything I can help you with? Is it anything anyone at the school can help you with? I know that there have been some changes in your life, and I'll try to be understanding . . . . . but you must do your work."

"Everything's okay." I try not to cry. "I promise I'll do the work. Don't make me take one of those papers home."

She thinks for a minute.

I sit there very quietly.

"Okay. For now, I won't make you take the paper home, but I do want you to make up your back work and turn in your book report tomorrow. Each day, your grade will go down one mark from what it would have been if you had turned it in on time."

I bite my lip. "Can I do extra credit?"

She shakes her head. "In this case, you may not. Extra credit's reserved for people who have tried their best and need an extra boost, or for people who are already doing their best and want to do more. YOU are not in either one of those categories."

She closes her marking book. "You have a chance to bring up your grade. Just make sure that you turn in all of your missing work."

I take the list of missing assignments that she hands me.

She continues. "Tomorrow, the class will be given a major project. Do well on it. I can't emphasize this highly enough. It will help bring up your grade for the marking period and will show me that you're serious about doing well."

I nod.

I, Amber Brown, may not be serious about a lot of things, but I am serious about this.

Chapter
Eleven

YOUR ASSIGNMENT: Giving Directions

Be prepared to give directions
to the class. Be logical. Be concise.
You may show how to build, make,
or do something (for example, you
may show how to build a fort,
make a dress, do karate, play an
instrument). Your directions must
be clear.

In addition to giving directions,

create something original concerning what you are explaining (e.g., making a poster, a film, or a computer program).

Your presentation can take between five and fifteen minutes.

I look at the assignment.

I have no idea what to do.

"Think about it," Mrs. Holt tells the class. "Tomorrow, let me know what you will be doing."

"How-To" . . . . . What does she want from me? What can I do to get the best grade possible? What will impress Mrs. Holt?

How to do . . . . . . I look around the room to try to come up with ideas. . . .

How to redecorate the classroom . . . How to stop Fredrich Allen from picking his nose and chewing it . . . . . How to crochet those ugly dolls that cover toilet-

paper rolls . . . . How to keep
from having to get a list of daily assignments
signed by my mother . . . How to find time
to do this project while I'm still finishing my
makeup work . . . .
. . . . . How to have a worry attack about
school . . . . How to not have a worry attack
about school . . . . How to come
up with a great idea for this project.

"Can we work together on the project?"
Naomi asks.

Mrs. Holt shakes her head no.

My brain hurts from trying to think up a
good project.

I start to doodle and write on my note-
book.

I must, I must, I must improve
my grades.
I better, I better, before I have
to take home a letter.

Maybe I should just let Mrs. Holt write the letter and get my mother all upset.

It would serve her right for going out with Max.

And then she would have to tell my father and then he would get all upset.

It would serve him right for going off to France and spending so little time with me.

It would serve them both right for getting divorced.

Amber Brown . . . . School Failure.

Sarah Thompson and Phil Brown . . . . . My Parents . . . . . . Family Failures.

The lunch bell rings.

I grab my lunch and head out the door. Brandi's already rushed out.

Some days she makes a fast dash to the girls' room.

She hates to ask for a pass in class.

One of the boys always says, "Hope everything comes out okay."

Mrs. Holt smiles at me. "Your book report was very good, Amber."

"Thanks. What'd I get?" I need to know.

"A C," she says. "It would have been a B if you'd turned it in on time."

Walking down the hall, I think about it . . . . *A C. Not a great grade, but not a bad one—"C" no evil.*

I laugh.

Sometimes I just make myself laugh.

Lunchroom.

Sit down with my friends.

"That little dirtbag." Tiffani opens her lunch.

This time, a Barbie arm is coming out of the lid of a yogurt.

"It's Cultured Barbie," I say.

"Maybe your project should be 'Things to Do with a Barbie Doll,'" Brandi suggests. "I bet that Howie could be a great help."

"I think . . ." Tiffani grins . . . . "it could be 'Things to Do to a Little Brother.' . . ."

"Brother Ka-Bobs," Bobby suggests. "Or what about . . . . . Little Brother Sushi?"

"EW . . . . . GROSS . . . . Stop it. I'm eating." Alicia makes gagging sounds.

Bobby can't stop . . . . "Microwave Brother . . . Brother McNuggets."

Bobby used to be an only child, just like me.

Then his mom got remarried and just had a baby boy.

I don't think he's overwhelmingly happy about not being an only child.

I, Amber Brown, can understand that.

"I know what I'm going to do for my project," Brandi says. "I'm going to show everyone how to do sign language."

"I know sign language," Bobby says.

"The only sign language you know could get you suspended." Jimmy starts to laugh.

They are so immature.

Brandi ignores them. "I'm going to teach some sign language and then show how a song we all know can be signed and interpreted. It's really beautiful."

"How do you know it?" I am surprised.

I thought I knew mostly everything about Brandi. I guess not.

When she moved here a year ago, Justin and I were still best friends, so we didn't really get to know each other until last month, and I guess it takes a while to learn everything.

She says, "Remember my cousin in California, the one who taught me to make the braids?"

I do remember. She made Brandi feel much better after she moved here and felt bad about not having any good, close friends.

"Well," Brandi continues, "her best friend is deaf, and they taught me to sign. I'm really good at it."

She moves her hands and signs something.

"What did you say?" I want to know.

She smiles. "I said, 'Do you want to share my brownie?' "

Licking my lips, I nod.

She makes a sign. "Yes."

I repeat the sign.

She hands me half her brownie.

"What's the sign for thank you?" I ask.

She shows me.

I make it and then start eating the brownie.

School brownies are not great.

My mom and I make really great ones.

And then I get an idea.

Chapter
Twelve

AMBER BROWNies.

Sitting on my bed, I start taking notes.

How to make AMBER BROWNies.

That's it.

I'm going to show how to make brownies.

Brownies . . . . . cakelike chocolate squares that are brown.

Not the Girl Scout kind of Brownies.

I know just making brownies is not going to be enough to get an A . . . . but I, Amber Brown, will do the best brownie project ever.

I'll explain . . . . the best explanation ever.

I'll experiment . . . . brownies with marshmallows, candy bits, fudge, tuna fish, to name a few ingredients.

I'll create an AMBER BROWNie cookbook.

I'll write to famous people and ask them for their recipes for brownies and I'll ask them to tell me brownie stories, memories.

I'll prepare a brownie questionnaire.

I'll create computer pictures of brownies.

I'll design Brownie Barf Bags for people who have eaten too many tuna brownies.

I'll make up a character and tell stories about him or her. . . . I don't know yet who it will be . . . . maybe Santa Brownie or the Easter Brownie or who knows.

I'll write a brownie song.

I'll get an *A*.

I'll also probably gain a zillion pounds and get brownie pimples from all of the research that I'm going to have to do.

But who cares . . . . . . I, Amber Brown, just have to get a great grade on this project.

Putting down my pen, I get up and rush downstairs.

"Mom!" I yell.

"Amber!" she yells back. "Stop the yelling."

I rush into the kitchen. "Mom, we've got to go shopping."

I stop rushing.

My mother is sitting with Max at the kitchen table.

He's not only sitting at the table, he's sitting in the chair where my dad used to sit.

"Hi, Amber." Max smiles at me.

"What are you doing here? I didn't know you were coming," I say.

"Amber." My mother does not look pleased. "You are being very rude."

"I didn't mean to be rude," I say. "I didn't know he was going to be here."

"Your mother didn't either. I was just

76

passing by and decided to drop in." He smiles at my mother.

I look at the flowers that are on the table that weren't there when I went upstairs about half an hour ago. Next to the vase is an envelope that says, *Sarah*.

Yeah, sure, I think . . . . . *Max was just passing by*.

"I lied about the just passing by," Max says.

"I figured." I grin at him.

It's hard not to grin at Max.

But I try.

I don't want this guy to think that he can drop in whenever he wants to.

"Mom." I turn to her. "I need to go shopping. It's for school. I've got to go to the grocery store."

"Amber, why didn't you tell me this morning when I went to the store? I have to do some work this afternoon." She shakes her head.

"But Mom . . . . . it's for school. I have to explain how to do something for school. I'm going to explain brownies. I NEED to go to the store. You don't want me to fail, do you?" I plead.

"No, I don't want you to fail." She sighs. "Explain what you need and when."

I tell them all of my ideas. "And I need to do the baking this weekend . . . either today or tomorrow . . . to test everything out, to make sure that it will work when I actually have to do it for the class. Please, oh please, oh please . . . . I just have to do a great job on this project. You have no idea how important this is to me. Please, oh please, oh please."

And I NEVER want my mother to find out just how important this really is to me, how I need to do well to make up for all the bad work and no work that I've been doing . . . . or not doing.

"Sarah, I can take Amber to the store

now. . . . . You can do some of your work while we're gone, and then I'll take you both out for pizza tonight." He turns from her to look at me. "Not brownie pizza, though."

Brownie pizza, I think. *It's possible.*

My mother looks at him. "Max Turner, I told you that I had to work tonight . . . . that we would spend tomorrow together. You're very sneaky."

I agree. Max is very sneaky.

I bet he's offering to help me just so that he gets to spend more time with my mother.

"Tomorrow," he says, "we can all bake the brownies."

"Are you still going to be here tomorrow?" I want to know.

My mother looks at me.

Then she looks at Max.

Then she looks back at me.

And then at Max. . . . .

Max looks at my mother.

79

And then he looks at me. "I would like to have pizza with you and your mom, and then I know she has work to do so I will leave right after dinner."

My mother smiles at him.

He smiles back.

There is too much smiling, much too much smiling going on around here.

He continues. "Since the plan was for Sarah and me to spend some time together tomorrow, I think we should use that time to help you with your project."

I wish he would stop being so nice . . . . . One of these days, I'm going to have to do something terrible to him to make him lose his temper.

But not today. . . . . I need to go shopping.

Chapter
Thirteen

"Wagons Ho," I say, putting on my seat-belt.

"Wagons Ho" is something my aunt Pam always says when we go someplace. It's become kind of a family thing to say at the beginning of some journeys.

I can't believe I've said it to Max, who is definitely not family. I wish I could take it back . . . but can't figure out how to do that . . . . so I think about taking it . . . . . . backward . . . that would be . . . . . . Oh Snogaw.

"Oh Snogaw," I say softly.

"What?" Max asks as he backs out of the driveway.

"Never mind." I shrug.

This is the first time I've been alone with Max . . . . and I've got a lot to tell him . . . . and a lot to ask.

I change the subject. "Do you have any kids? Have you ever been married? Do you want to marry my mom? Do you know that even though my mom and dad are divorced, there is a very good chance that they're going to get back together . . . . . that they're just taking a break from each other . . . . kind of like recess?"

Max keeps driving, without saying a word.

It makes me nervous that he's not saying anything.

I've never had to meet anyone that my mother was dating . . . mostly because she didn't go out on dates for a long time after my dad left . . . and then because she said I didn't have to meet anyone unless it was serious, and now she's made me meet Max, so I know this must be serious.

So I continue. "Do you know that my mom and I have been very happy just living together by ourselves? We like it that way . . . . . until my dad moves back from France. Then we're going to all live together again . . . . my mom . . . . my dad . . . and me."

I wait for him to say something.

Just before we get to the supermarket, Max pulls into the Dairy Queen, my favorite ice cream place.

"You can't bribe me," I say.

The car stops, and Max says, "I know. I just think that we should talk, and when I talk with friends, we often discuss things over a cup of coffee. I didn't think that we should have coffee."

"I don't drink coffee," I tell him. "I don't know a lot of nine-year-olds who do. . . .

My friend Justin used to like coffee ice cream, though."

We get out of the car and order ice cream.

I get two scoops in a dish, chocolate chip mint and vanilla fudge.

He gets coffee ice cream.

We sit down.

I mush up my ice cream and wait for the answers.

Chocolate chip mint and vanilla fudge mushed together looks pretty gross.

Max starts. "I've never been married. I don't have any kids. My niece, my sister's daughter, Jade, and I are very close. Jade's father left before she was born, so I've been like a father to her. She's six."

"My dad would never do anything like that," I say.

Max looks at me and nods. "I know. Your mom has told me how much he loves you."

"He does," I say, and then ask, "Do you want to marry my mom?"

Max looks at me. "Amber, your mother and I have only been dating since this summer . . . a few months. We're not talking about getting married . . . but when WE do talk about it, I'm sure that your mother will talk to you."

"You said WHEN, not IF." I let my ice cream drip down my chin.

He looks surprised. "I guess I did. . . . . That's very interesting."

"My dad will be back soon," I remind him.

"Your mother said that he was going to try to move back. But Amber, I think you should talk to your mother about this . . . . . . about whether or not they're going to get back together."

I stand up. "We better go shopping now."

He stands up too, picks up a napkin, and

wipes the dripping ice cream off my face.

"Are you being nice to me because you want me to like you?" I ask.

"I'm being nice to you because I'm basically nice." He grins. "And, yes, I do want you to like me. But I'm not going to like it if you do stuff to try to mess things up between your mother and me . . . . but I will try to understand . . . . and to remember how rotten I was to the man who eventually became my stepfather."

Stepfather. I don't like that word.

"Would you tell me some of the things that you did to him?" I want to know because that information might be useful someday.

He laughs. "Not on your life. . . . Why should I tell you? So that you can use them on me? Do you think I'm nuts?"

I just smile at him.

"Don't answer that." He smiles back.

"You can tell me. Come on. I thought

you said you're a nice guy. It would be nice to tell me."

"I'm not that nice." He shakes his head.

One of these days, I'm going to get him to tell me . . . . and then I'm going to do the same thing to him . . . . . whatever it was . . . . I don't want to make all of this too easy for Max.

I'm beginning to like him . . . but I don't want to like him too much. . . . After all, what if he decides to stick around . . . or what if I like him a lot and then he decides to leave?

We get into the car, go to the supermarket, and get a cart.

The shopping begins.

We play supermarket basketball, lobbing all of the ingredients, except for the eggs and oil, into the cart. We get more points the farther we throw the items.

We also get strange looks from some of the other shoppers.

Then we play Guess the Weight.

Max picks up an item. Then he hands it to me and we both guess how much it weighs.

Then he takes it over to the fruit-weighing machine and we see who wins.

I'm ahead, fifteen to seven.

"Two points!" I yell as I throw a bag of marshmallows into the cart.

Max pretends to guard it, but it goes in.

There's loud cheering. It's the Nicholson brothers, Danny, Ryan, and Kyle. Danny, who's in third grade, gives Max a high five and says to me, "Amber, your dad is so much fun. . . . . ."

Max smiles.

I yell, "He's not my dad!" Danny looks really surprised that I yelled like that.

Max looks sad.

I look at both of them and then I say to Danny, "He's my mother's friend."

And then I add, "And he's my friend too."

Max looks happy again.

And I feel good that I've said that he's my friend.

I also feel a little guilty.

I'm not sure that my father would like it if he knew about Max and if he knew that I said that he's my friend.

Max throws a bag of jelly beans into the cart. "Two points."

By the time we get to the checkout counter, we have a tie score.

No one wins.

No one loses.

Chapter
Fourteen

It's Brownie Baking Day, and Max is back again.

The ingredients that I put in the refrigerator yesterday are on the table, and I'm emptying the rest of the stuff out of the bag.

"I don't believe you two." My mother shakes her head.

"Believe us." Max comes up behind her and puts his arms around her waist.

She doesn't move away or anything.

I continue to put the ingredients on the table.

"When you two came back last night, I

should have looked through the shopping bags." She shakes her head again.

Sprinkles . . . . M&M's . . . . Reese's Pieces . . . . . marshmallows . . . . gumdrops . . . . slivered almonds . . . walnuts . . . a can of tuna fish . . . a Mars bar . . . a bag of potato chips . . . . . Cheez Doodles . . . Gummi

worms, a bar of white chocolate . . . Good & Plenty . . . . candy false teeth . . . . . candy corn . . . strawberry Twizzlers . . . . Cheerios . . . peanut butter . . . . . grape jelly . . . . plus all of the regular stuff that goes into plain brownies. . . . . . .

"This is disgusting." My mother shakes her head . . . again.

"I know." I grin. "It's great."

"I'm never sending the two of you out shopping together, never again." My mother just keeps shaking her head.

She's beginning to look like one of those bobbing dolls that some people have in the back window of their cars.

Her head would probably be falling off if she knew *how* Max and I shopped.

Max.

He's put one hand over my mother's eyes and is feeding her some of the ingredients and making her guess what they are.

Marshmallows are easy for her.

So are the nuts, candy corn, and Twizzlers.

Max puts an M&M in my mother's mouth.

"This one's a piece of cake," my mother says.

"No. Wrong. It's an M&M." Max takes his hand away from my mother's eyes and gives her a kiss.

I, Amber Brown, could have told him that "a piece of cake" in my mother's language means that it's super easy . . . but something tells me that Max already knows that.

I, Amber Brown, can also tell him that I'm not too sure about how I feel about him kissing my mom.

My mother starts to laugh, and then she looks over at me.

She looks a little guilty, sort of like she knows that I am not crazy about them kissing each other.

I clap my hands. "Come on, everyone, let's turn on the oven and do some preheating."

My mother and Max both laugh.

I don't get it.

"What's so funny?" I want to know.

"Nothing." My mother moves away from Max and puts the oven on.

Max puts out the cupcake papers, which we're using instead of baking pans so that we can make individual brownies with different stuff in them.

"What's so funny?" I repeat.

"Nothing," my mother repeats.

I make a face.

"It was a private joke," my mother tells me.

I don't think that Max and my mother should be having private jokes, not so soon.

I hate it when adults laugh in front of you and then say that it's a private joke.

It's kind of like when you're real little and

grown-ups spell in front of you.

And it's not fair.

Parents always make kids tell when the kids have a private joke.

And teachers always say things like, "Amber, would you like to share that with the rest of the class?"

And then if you say, "No, I really wouldn't," they make you do it anyway or they give you detention.

"The oven's heating up." My mother smiles. "Let's get this show on the road."

We get started.

Max pretends to be a French chef . . . "And now for zee eggs . . . ."

My mother starts singing, "Hi-ho, hi-ho . . . . . it's off to work we go," and she pretends to be one of the Seven Dwarfs . . . . Dopey, I think.

Max says that he's the eighth dwarf, Hungry.

I pretend to be the grown-up, lecturing

them on taking the job seriously and telling them not to eat so much of the batter (which I keep doing).

Our faces are covered with chocolate.

Max has just made a tuna–jelly-bean brownie.

My mother looks at his brownie and makes retching noises.

She's decorated her marshmallow brownie with sprinkles.

I'm filling my brownie with Gummi
worms crawling through it and over it.

The phone rings.

It's my father.

Chapter Fifteen

"Hi, honey." My dad sounds like he's practically next door, not all the way in Paris, France. "How are you?"

"Fine," I say.

"What are you doing?"

I don't want to mention the good time that Max, Mom, and I are having, so I say, "Not much."

"I miss you so much. Do you miss me?"

"Yes, Daddy, I miss you bunches."

I sit in the living room, talking on the phone.

My mother and Max are in the kitchen.

"I miss you," I repeat.

"How much?" He's smiling . . . I can tell by his voice.

"This much." I spread my arms as far as I can while holding the phone between my shoulder and my ear.

"And how much is that?" he says, playing the I-love-you-this-much game we've always played with each other.

"To the next universe," I tell him.

"To the farthest galaxy," he tells me. "I love you and miss you that much."

I try to imagine what he's looking like at the other end.

I haven't seen my father for a couple of months, not since last summer when my aunt Pam took me to London, England.

I was supposed to visit him in Paris for a week but then I got the stupid chicken pox and he came to London instead.

We only got to spend a couple of days together.

And even though we talk on the phone every week, it's not the same.

Just before I start to tell him some stuff about me, he starts talking about what he's been doing, how he went to Euro Disney with a friend of his from work . . . . and with her little boy.

I was supposed to go to Euro Disney with him last summer.

The stupid chicken pox.

All I have is a Euro Disney sweatshirt that my dad sent me before I even went to England.

"Who is your friend, the one with the little boy?" I twirl the phone wire. "Did her husband go too?"

There's a pause for a minute, and then my dad says, "They're divorced. You know, Amber, you'd really like Judith and her son, Todd. He's the cutest little six-year-old. I've been spending a lot of time with them lately."

I think, *Here we go again*.

I'm just getting used to Max. Now I have to find out about Judith and Todd.

I say nothing for a minute, and then, "Cuter than when I was six?"

"No one was cuter than my Amber," he says.

My stomach starts to hurt.

I wonder if I've been eating too much brownie batter.

My father continues. "Maybe you can come over here during Christmas vacation and meet them. . . . . I'm sure that you'll really like them . . . and we'll finally be able to spend some time together."

There's so much to think about.

I'm getting a headache.

A headache . . . . . a stomachache . . . . maybe it's the attack of a killer flu that suddenly attacks nine-year-old girls who have eaten too much brownie batter. Maybe it's a telephone virus.

I don't want to meet this stupid Judith person and her stupid little dweeb son, who get to spend time with my father in Euro Disney when I hardly ever get to see him.

Why did my father even have to mention them?

This is my phone call, my time with him.

"Amber, I really miss you so much. Tell me what you've been doing. I feel like I'm missing so much."

"You could move back," I tell him.

"I can't, not yet." He sighs. "We've been through this already. It's my job . . . . and I need to earn money. I've got a lot of extra expenses."

"Maybe you'd have more money if you weren't taking strangers to Euro Disney."

"Amber, don't be silly," he says.

I hate to be told that I'm being silly when I tell him how I feel.

"Look. I've got to be going now. Mom and I are in the middle of making brownies with her friend Max. He took me shopping yesterday. We're all having so much fun."

There's silence at the other end.

I continue. "In a couple of weeks, there's going to be a carnival at school. I'm probably going to be very busy going to that with Mom and Max. You'll probably be very busy doing something with Judith and her little dweeb . . . . so if you don't call, it'll be okay."

"Amber." He raises his voice. "Stop this. Stop it right now. Don't be angry. Be reasonable. I only mentioned Judith because I want you to know about my life . . . so that we can stay close. I'm sorry if I've done this the wrong way."

"You could have asked about my schoolwork," I say. "Actually, I've been getting into trouble at school, not doing my schoolwork."

There's silence at the other end for a minute, and then he says, "Why didn't your mother call me to talk about this?"

"She's handling it," I lie. "She didn't have to spend her money on a long-distance phone call. And anyway, she talks to Max about stuff like that now."

"Amber, when we've finished talking, I want to speak to your mother."

"She and Max are watching that the brownies don't burn. And I've got to go back now and help them. Well, it's been nice talking to you."

I hang up the phone.

I hang up the phone before we even have our kissing contest, which we always have at the end of a call. That's where we make kissing sounds into the phone until one of us gets tired and quits and the other one wins.

No kissing contest this time . . . . . no winners.

I can feel myself start to cry.

The phone rings.

I run upstairs.

Chapter Sixteen

My Dad Book . . . .

I open the top drawer of my dresser, take it out, and sit down on my bed to think about the best ways to destroy it.

I could feed it into the garbage disposal.

I could take each picture out of the book and rip it into tiny, tiny, minuscule pieces.

I could take a picture of him and add drawings to it of what I think Judith and the little dweeb look like . . . and then I can rip it into tiny, tiny, minuscule pieces.

I could blow my nose on some of the

pictures . . . . put a little snot across my father's face.

I could . . . . but I can't.

I don't want to destroy my Dad Book.

Opening it, I look at some of the pictures . . . . . . the time my dad and I won the father-daughter race at my school. I wonder who's going to win it this year.

Maybe they'll have a mother's boyfriend–daughter race this year and Max and I can win it.

Max.

I don't know what to think about Max either.

I don't know why everything had to become so complicated.

There's a knock on the door.

It's my mother.

I know.

Now's the time for the mother-daughter talk . . . how it's not easy for any of us

. . . . . how my parents have to make new lives . . . how we all have to try to be flexible and understanding . . . . how while they don't love each other, they'll always love me.

I don't say anything.

There's another knock on the door, and then my mother walks in and sits down with me on my bed.

"I know . . . . . . you love me . . . . you have to make a new life . . . . . Max is a wonderful person . . . . . . you and Dad may hate each other's guts but you'll always love me." I look at her.

"Well, I guess that's it." My mother stands up.

She sits down again. "No. Actually, there is more. Do you want to say it . . . or should I say the rest of things that need to be said . . . . . and need to be done?"

"I think I said everything." I shrug.

She picks up the Dad Book and opens it.
The page she has turned to is a picture of
my dad, with me sitting on Santa's knees.
She smiles at it and then looks at me.

"Amber, your dad is very upset that you hung up on him like that."

"What do you care? You hate his guts." I make a face.

She thinks for a minute. "Some of his guts I hate . . . . but, Amber, I don't hate all of his guts."

I laugh. "Just how many of his guts do you hate?"

She shakes her head. "Don't try to make me laugh. . . . This is serious. . . . Don't make a joke out of this. I know you're upset. Your father told me what's upsetting you. . . . Amber, you have a right to your feelings . . . . but you know that you have to be open to changes."

"They're not *my* changes. They're yours . . . . yours and Dad's. . . ." I am not laughing.

"You're making changes too. . . . You're getting older. . . . . You like different things

113

. . . . You even look different. Your dad and I have to get used to your changes too."

"But I'm a kid. I *have* to grow and change and be different."

"So do we." My mother is trying to be

calm. "Everyone in the world has to grow and change in some ways."

"But everyone doesn't have to like the changes." I pout. "You don't like everything I do."

She pretends to pout. "And you don't like everything *I* do."

I pout more. "I'm sick of having to hear this all the time."

"And I'm sick of having to say it all the time." She makes a super pouting face and then she smiles. "Amber Brown, you have to get used to change."

We both are quiet for a minute, and then she says, "And what's this about you're still not doing your schoolwork? Did you mean what you told your father?"

Great. I try to work really hard so that she doesn't find out and then I tell on myself.

I tell her what's going on.

I explain about how Mrs. Holt won't give me extra credit.

"She's right, you know." My mother pats me on the head.

It makes me nuts when she pats me on the head.

"But I want extra credit. . . . . I want a gold star for all the stuff I'm going through."

"It's called living. . . . Everyone goes through real stuff. . . . No one gets a gold star for doing what they should be doing."

"This is one of those great truths." I look at her. "One of those mother-daughter moments I'm always going to remember. . . . . ."

"And cherish . . . . ." my mother says, and then she laughs. "And then someday you will be saying the same things to *your* daughter."

"If I ever get married and have a kid, I'll never get divorced."

"I hope you never have to." My mother looks at me and then gives me a hug.

I hug back.

Then we look at each other.

"Mom." I hold her hand. "If I can't have a gold star .... can I at least have a brownie?"

She squeezes my hand and nods. "Let's go down and get some before Max eats them all."

"I bet he's not eating the tuna-fish-and-jelly-bean brownie."

"I bet he's not," she agrees. "And I bet you don't either."

We get up and go downstairs.

On the way, I think of a slogan to use on my project.

With AMBER BROWNies, You Get Your Just Desserts.

Chapter
Seventeen

Progress Report

After some initial problems,
Amber is doing quite well at school
in her subject areas. She is turning
in good work on time. Amber still
needs to work very hard in math,
but I can tell that she is trying.

Her attitude is much better . . .
and her AMBER BROWNie report
was a delight . . . . and quite
tasteful!

Amber deserves credit for doing her best.

I look forward to watching her progress for the rest of the year.